Contents

KU-513-047

What is winter?

spring

summer

autumn

winter

There are four seasons every year.

Winter is one of the four seasons.

When is winter?

spring

summer

winter

autumn

The four seasons follow a pattern.

Winter comes after autumn.

The weather in winter

It can be cold in winter.

It can snow in winter.

What can we see in winter?

In winter we can see people in gloves.

In winter we can see people in coats.

In winter we can see trees with
no leaves.

In winter we can see ice.

In winter we can see sledges.

In winter we can see ice skaters.

In winter we can see snowmen.

In winter we can see hot drinks.

In winter we can see decorations.

In winter we can see lights.

In winter some birds are hungry.

In winter some animals sleep.

Which season comes next?

Which season comes after winter?

22

Picture glossary

decoration something used to make things look good

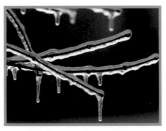

ice frozen water. Ice can be cold, hard, and slippery.

pattern happening in the same order

Index

Notes for parents and teachers
Before reading
Talk to the children about the four seasons of the year: spring, summer, autumn, winter. Ask the children in which season people celebrate Bonfire Night and Diwali. In which season do people give Easter eggs? In which season do people start the New Year? In which season is the weather the hottest? Listen to a few minutes of *Winter* from Vivaldi's *Four Seasons*. Tell the children to close their eyes and think about the following images of winter: snow on the ground, frozen ponds and puddles, people dressed up warmly.

After reading
• Make a puppet snowman. Cut a snowman outline (three connected circles) out of foam. Cut a hat, two eyes, and three "buttons" out of black gummed paper. Cut a nose out of orange gummed paper. Stick them on the snowman outline. Glue or tape a drinking straw to the back of the snowman.
• Play the *Snowman's Dance* from the film *The Snowman* and encourage children to dance their snowmen in time to the music.
• Create a snowy scene. Help the children to draw a snowy scene on to black paper using wax crayons. Paint over the scene with white paint. The paint will not cover the crayon and will give the effect of snow covering the ground. While the paint is still wet, scatter white or silver glitter.